Suzie Squirrel

Dave and Pat Sargent are longtime residents of Prairie Grove, Arkansas. Dave, a fourth-generation dairy farmer, began writing in early December 1990, and Pat, a former teacher, began writing shortly after. They enjoy the outdoors and have a real love for animals.

Suzie Squirrel

By

Dave and Pat Sargent

Illustrated by
Jeane Huff

Ozark Publishing, Inc.
P.O. Box 228
Prairie Grove, AR 72753

Library of Congress cataloging-in-publication data

Sargent, Dave, 1941—
   Susie Squirrel / by Dave and Pat Sargent ; illustrated by Jeane Huff.
     p. cm.
   Summary: Suzie Squirrel gets into trouble whenher friend Sissy persuades her to do as she pleases and criticizes others.
   ISBN 1-56763-394-3 (hardcover). — ISBN 1-56763-395-1 (pbk.)
    [1. Squirrels—Fiction. 2. Behavior—Fiction.]
   I. Sargent, Pat, 1936—   .II. Huff, Jeane, 1946— ill. III. Title.
   PZ7.S2465Su 1998   97-26508
   [Fic]—dc21   CIP
                               AC

Printed in the United States of America

iv

Inspired by

two pet squirrels I had as a girl. My dad found them in the woods, alone and hungry. He said their mother must have been shot or had died of other causes. I fed them warm milk with an eye dropper. I kept those two little squirrels for five years. My mother made me turn them loose when they started running up and down her window curtains, tearing them. I cried that day.

Dedicated to

children who love to walk through the woods and watch squirrels play.

Foreword

Suzie Q is a little squirrel who loves to play. She gets into trouble when her young friend, Sissy, a little red squirrel, convinces her that she should do as she pleases. Suzie Q learns a bad habit from Sissy. She learns to criticize others. And that's when her problems begin.

Contents

Suzie Squirrel

If you would like to have the authors of the Animal Pride Series visit your school, free of charge, call 1-800-321-5671 or 1-800-960-3876.

One

Captured

"Suzie! Where are you, girl?" Mama Squirrel called. She had looked high and low for Suzie Q all morning long. Not one trace of the feisty little squirrel could she find.

"Now, where could that girl be? She's not in the nest in our hollow tree. She's not playing under the tree. She's not out gathering acorns. She's not out gathering pecans. She's not out gathering walnuts. What is she doing that's more important than helping her brothers and sisters and her mama and daddy store up food for the coming winter?" Mama asked, shaking her head.

Mama Squirrel was beginning to worry about Suzie Q. Suzie Q's cousin Sissy, a little red squirrel, had been coming over often to play, and Sissy didn't have good manners.
Now, Mama Squirrel knew that she should keep Suzie Q away from Sissy, but she didn't want to make Sissy's mama mad, because Sissy's mama could be downright mean when she got mad. She criticized the way Mama Squirrel raised her babies. And to make matters worse, young Sissy was just like her mama!

Sissy criticized everyone and scolded Suzie Q's brothers, whether they really deserved it or not. And

Suzie Q played with Sissy all the time. Yes, Sissy was a very bad influence on her sweet little Suzie Q. Mama Squirrel shook her tail.

With her large, bushy tail curled up over her head, Mama Squirrel sat in the top of the big, tall, hollow tree, her eyes scanning the ground below. Her large, bushy tail kept the hot sun off her head. Suddenly, she saw two young squirrels scampering in and out and around the tree trunks below.

One of the little squirrels had gray fur on her back and whitish fur on her underparts. Yes, that was her little Suzie Q. The other squirrel had reddish fur on her back and white fur on her underparts. She was smaller than Suzie Q. That would be Sissy.

"Suzie Q!" Mama Squirrel called, louder than before. "It's time to come home now. It's time to eat, then we must gather and store some more food for the coming winter."

Suzie Q stopped and looked up at the top of the tree. She saw her mama sitting in the top of the tree shaking her tail. Mama Squirrel always shook her tail when she meant business.

Suzie Q turned to Sissy and said, "I have to go home now, Sissy. We can play again tomorrow."

Sissy frowned. "Why do you have to go home, Suzie Q? I don't go home when my mama calls me. Mamas are too bossy!"

Suzie Q stared at young Sissy. Not mind Mama? Why, she would never think of disobeying her mama.

Shame on Sissy. Mama was right. Sissy was a bad girl.

Suzie Q ran toward the hollow tree, then stopped. She looked back at Sissy. Maybe Sissy was right about Mama Squirrel and everyone else. She looked up. Mama Squirrel was shaking her tail again.

Suzie Q said, "You're right, Sissy. Come on. Let's play some more. I'm not ready to go home, not yet. I've decided to be like you. I'm going to start doing just as I please beginning right now!"

Suddenly, Suzie heard Mama's chirp, whistle, and dreaded chirrrr! To little Suzie Q that meant *danger*! She didn't know which way to run. The grass was tall. She couldn't see. A big paw came out of the tall green grass and flattened her to the ground.

Long sharp teeth grabbed the nape of Suzie Q's neck, and she felt herself being flung from side to side as a black and tan coonhound with long ears carried her off.

Two

Barney's Prize

When Barney the Bear Killer got to the back gate, he stopped and waited for the girls to notice him. Finally, Amber looked his way. She ran over to the gate to let him in.

"What you got there, Barney? Your supper too heavy for you to jump over the gate like you usually do?"

The girls stood staring at the furry thing with the big black eyes and the long, bushy tail that Barney had in his mouth. It was wiggling and squirming, trying to get free.

Barney had a look of triumph on his face. He had finally captured something that he'd had his eye on for some time. His face changed when he noticed the soft, mushy looks on the girls' faces. He lowered his head, then sat little Suzie Q on the ground at the girls' feet.

Suzie Q ruffled her fur out, shook her long, bushy tail, then let out a string of chirps and whistles, scolding Barney good! The girls squealed with delight.

Before Suzie Q could regain her composure, Amber reached down and picked her up, then ran into the house to show her mama what Barney had brought home. This was going to be a great pet!

When Amber walked in with a little squirrel, Molly's eyes flew open. "How did you catch that cute little squirrel?" she asked.

Farmer John, knowing how ole Barney loved to watch squirrels play, didn't ask such a question because he figured he already knew the answer. A big grin covered his face.

Farmer John went to the back door and looked down at ole Barney, who was sitting at the screen door, watching Amber with his prize. Didn't seem fair. Barney caught it. Barney should get to eat it.

Farmer John said, "Better give it back to Barney, Amber. That little squirrel will make him a nice supper. He'll finish it off in short order."

Amber held Suzie Q close. She glanced toward the back door. There stood Barney the Bear Killer with that look of anticipation on his face.

Amber said, "Oh, please let me keep it, Daddy. I want it for a pet. Don't let Barney eat the little thing. Please, Daddy!"

"And what about next week or next month?" Farmer John asked. "Dogs like squirrel meat, Amber, and ole Barney's a good hunter."

Farmer John looked at Molly. "What do you think, Molly?" he asked.

Molly smiled at Amber, then said, "I think the girls should keep the little squirrel for a pet. It's not very old and could be easily tamed."

Molly's face took on a sad look. As she stood there, she lowered her head. Everyone noticed the sad look that had crossed her face.

"What is it, Mama? What's wrong?" Amber asked.

"Oh, I was just remembering," Molly said, "remembering all the fun I had with my little squirrels. I raised two of them. My daddy brought them home from a hunting trip one day."

"How long did you keep them, Mama? And where did you keep them?" April asked.

"I kept them in my room or tried to," Molly answered. "They got out of my room so many times, Mama finally said I could let them run around the house as long as they didn't tear up anything."

Ashley had been standing there, taking it all in. She asked, "Did they sleep with you, Mama? Did they sleep in your bed?"

Molly smiled. "No, they didn't sleep in my bed. My daddy made them a cage, and they slept in their cage at night. We would not have been able to sleep if they had been running around the house. Besides, Mama did a lot of baking, and there were usually pies, cakes, corn bread, or biscuits sitting on the kitchen table."

"But why the sad look when you started talking about them, Mama?" Amber asked.

"Oh, I had lots of fun raising them," Molly answered. "That sad look you girls saw was from my remembering the day they ran up Mama's curtains and tore them. She made me take the squirrels deep into the woods and turn them loose."

The girls stared at their mama. "She made you turn them loose?" they all asked at once.

Molly shrugged her shoulders. "I had to turn them loose because I had not done what Mama said. I had not kept an eye on them. I was not responsible enough."

The girls considered this. They knew what responsibility was. They knew what the word meant.

Farmer John grinned. "Well, I guess it won't hurt anything if you keep the little squirrel for a while. How long you keep it depends on how well you take care of it."

The girls squealed with delight. They ran to their room and shut the door, then placed the little squirrel on the floor. Suzie Q looked around the room, then jumped on the bed, scampered across it, and jumped for the open window, hitting the screen.

It chattered and chirped, scolding the girls and that window screen! The girls fell on the bed, laughing. What a great pet this was going to be!

Three

Sharp Teeth Snap!

Suzie Q sat on the windowsill. Outside, white stuff was falling.

Suzie Q was just sitting there, wondering what her mama and her brothers and sisters were doing. She was beginning to get homesick, and she was really wanting to go home. That's what she would do if she got the chance. If the little girls took her outside today to play in that fluffy white stuff that was falling, she would run away home; that is, if she could find the way.

Right after lunch, it stopped snowing, and the sun popped out. The girls grabbed their coats and snow boots and began putting their boots on. They hurried out the door, squirrel and all. Barney tolerated the squirrel, only because the girls were always near, but given the chance, he knew he could do away with that furry little thing in nothing flat.

Molly made a pan of hot cocoa, then called the girls in. They drank it fast, then ran outside.

Ashley looked all around, then asked, "Where's the squirrel? I don't see it." The girls' faces took on looks of disbelief. Oh, no! They had forgotten to take it inside with them. "Oh, my gosh!" Amber exclaimed. "Where's Barney?"

The little squirrel was gone, and Barney the Bear Killer was gone. The girls just knew that Barney had eaten the squirrel and was asleep somewhere letting his meal digest.

Out in the middle of the field, Suzie Q was running fast, heading straight to the tree where her mama, brothers, and sisters lived. And Barney was right behind her. He didn't want to lose his prize again.

Suzie Q knew that ole Barney would soon catch her if she didn't reach the woods so she could climb a tree. Why had she listened to Sissy? She realized that if she hadn't starting thinking critical thoughts about her mama, she wouldn't be in this boat right now. She didn't want to be critical like Sissy. She had learned her lesson.

Suzie Q was really tired. She had never in her life run so fast—if she could just make it to the trees. Just when she was ready to drop, she reached the edge of the woods. As she scampered up the closest tree, she felt Barney's hot breath on her back. She reached the first limb and made a desperate leap! Behind her, she heard sharp teeth snap.

Ole Barney the Bear Killer sat at the foot of that tree for a good ten minutes before Suzie Q noticed a tree close by. She decided to jump. She knew if she missed she would hit the ground, but she had to try. She gathered her tiny muscles and jumped with her legs spread out!

Suzie Q's front feet touched a limb, then horrified, she felt herself falling. A low branch with lots of tiny limbs and leaves caught her. She lay still for a long time before she moved. She looked down. That ole coonhound was leaving, but he kept looking back at the tree.

Barney trotted toward home. He sure didn't want to be late for the evening milking. Farmer John should be getting the cows in about now, and he might need help.

Susie Q finally reached home. And even though her cousin Sissy came often to play, Suzie Q was very careful about believing the things Sissy said. Sissy had not changed. She still criticized everyone.

Suzie Q wanted to be happy. She was, too. She minded her mama. She did her part to help her family. And she was never again critical of others.

Suzie Q learned to stay out in the open, unless, of course, it was squirrel hunting season, and she always kept a sharp eye out for that ole black and tan coonhound.

Four

Squirrel Facts

Squirrels are furry-tailed animals with large, black eyes and rounded ears. Many squirrels are very lively animals with long, bushy tails.

Squirrels may scamper about the ground or in trees. Tree squirrels are often seen in woodlands and parks. They include gray squirrels, fox squirrels, red squirrels, and flying squirrels.

The flying squirrel has a fold of skin that stretches from its front leg to its rear leg on each side of its body. This skin acts like the wings of a glider, and gives the animal "lift." Some flying squirrels can glide more than one hundred and fifty feet, but fifty to sixty feet is a more usual distance. Unlike other tree squirrels, flying squirrels are usually active only at night. They live throughout the United States and Canada.

Many kinds of squirrels have short tails and never climb trees. They are called ground squirrels. These include chipmunks, marmots, prairie dogs, and woodchucks.

Squirrels live throughout the world except in southern South America, Madagascar, and Australia.

One of the smallest squirrels is the African pygmy squirrel, found in western Africa. It weighs about one-half ounce and is three inches long without the two-inch tail.

The largest is the marmot. It weighs up to twenty pounds and grows as long as thirty inches, including a ten-inch tail.

There are over three hundred kinds of squirrels. Squirrels are one of the largest families of rodents (gnawing animals). Like other rodents, squirrels have chisel-like front teeth. Many kinds of squirrels, especially tree squirrels and chipmunks, are easy to tame. They may learn to take nuts and other food from a person's hand. But even a tame squirrel may bite or scratch a person and cause a serious wound.

The word squirrel comes from two Greek words that mean *shadow tail*. At first, the word may have been used only for tree squirrels. The large, bushy tails curl over their backs and seem to keep them in the shade.

Most kinds of tree squirrels are active, noisy animals. They seem to scold one another continually in a variety of loud chirps, whistles, and noises that sound somewhat like *chirrrr.*

Many squirrels have two homes: a warm, permanent one, and, for hot days, a temporary one that is cool. The permanent home may be a den in an old hollow tree trunk, or a really sturdy nest built on a branch.

In Great Britain, a squirrel's nest is called a dray. A squirrel's den is lined with dry leaves and strips of bark. In winter, several squirrels may share a den.

A permanent nest is made of layers of twigs and leaves packed together to keep out rain, snow, and wind. A temporary nest is only a loose pile of twigs and leaves. It soon falls apart, and a squirrel may have to build several each summer.

Squirrels move about easily in trees or on rooftops or telephone wires. They spread their legs straight out and leap from place to place. Squirrels use their bushy tails to keep their balance when they jump.

Squirrels eat berries, fruits, corn, mushrooms, nuts, and seeds. They spend much time searching for food. A squirrel is especially busy in autumn, when it gathers food for the winter. Squirrels store food in holes in the ground, in trees, or in their dens.

Red squirrels are famous for the many pine cones they cut and store for food. A red squirrel may cut more than a hundred cones from a tree in an hour. Then the animal rushes to the ground, gathers the cones, and hides them. The hiding place may be a hollow tree stump. Or the squirrel may pile the cones around a stone or a log and cover them with leaves. When winter comes, the squirrel may have three to ten bushels of cones.

A female squirrel carries her young in her body for thirty-six to forty-five days before she gives birth. She may give birth twice a year, and usually from two to six young are born at a time.

Newborn squirrels have no fur, and their eyes are closed. Flying squirrels and red squirrels may open their eyes twenty-six to twenty-eight days after birth, but little gray squirrels may take as long as thirty-seven days. When squirrels are five to eight weeks old, they have all their fur and begin to search for their own food. They begin having their own families when they near a year old.

Humans are the greatest enemies of squirrels. People hunt most kinds of squirrels for sport, but they hunt tree squirrels for their meat and fur.

Other enemies include bobcats, cats, coyotes, dogs, and foxes. These squirrels race for the nearest tree when an enemy comes near.

Squirrels may live for two to six years in the wild. Some have lived for fifteen years in captivity.